BEN 10
ULTIMATE ALIEN
™

SCIENCE FRICTION

ISBN 978-0-545-17719-1

CARTOON NETWORK, the logo, Ben 10 Ultimate Alien, and all related
characters and elements are trademarks of and © 2010 Cartoon Network.
Published by Scholastic Inc.
SCHOLASTIC and associated logos are trademarks and/or registered
trademarks of Scholastic Inc.

12 11 10 9 8 7 6 5 4 3 2 1   10 11 12 13 14 15/0

Illustrations by Min Sung Ku and Hi-Fi Design
Printed in the U.S.A.
First printing, September 2010

"Come on, Kevin," Cooper urged. "Just try it on. You'll look totally cool, I promise."

"Dude, I am not taking fashion advice from a guy wearing an orange jumpsuit," Kevin replied. "You look like a contestant on *America's Top Dork*."

"Maybe you'll look good in fur," teased Kevin's sometimes girlfriend, Gwen.

But Kevin was firm. "No way," he told Cooper. "I know I owe you one for helping me fix that Talkion transmitter, but when I agreed to go to this stupid sci-fi con with you, nobody said anything about a costume."

"I think this convention is going to be a good time," said Gwen's cousin, Ben. "Sci-fi movies are pretty cool."

"Of course you would say that," Kevin said. "Your whole life is like a sci-fi movie."

Cooper sighed. "Fine. But we've got to hurry before the lines get too long."

They walked inside the convention center. Sci-fi fans crowded the displays. Lots of them, like Cooper, wore costumes of their favorite movie and comic book characters.

Suddenly, a man pointed at Ben. "Look, everyone! It's Ben Tennyson, the guy who can turn into *real* aliens!"

"Uh-oh!" Ben said. Ever since word had gotten out on the Internet about his special powers, it was hard for him to go out without being recognized. Thinking fast, he grabbed the monster head from Cooper.

Ben ducked behind a booth and put on the monster head just in time. The crowd ran right past him.

"You look like a deranged teddy bear," Gwen said.
"At least I can blend in now," Ben pointed out.
Cooper was anxious to see the booth for *Alien Invasion*, a new movie coming out that summer. The booth was set up with movie props and models of the aliens. Cooper got an autograph from the film's star, Max Kane.

Kevin picked up one of the prop weapons and rolled his eyes. "Look at those cheesy ray guns," he sneered. "Whoever made this movie doesn't know anything about aliens."

Cooper shook his head. "No way. This movie is going to be awesome."

Then Kevin noticed a strange-looking device among the props. He examined it, frowning.

"Wait a minute," he said. "This looks like real alien tech."

One of the workers from the booth walked by. Kevin grabbed her by the arm.

"Excuse me. Where did you get this?" he asked.

The girl shrugged. "It all came from the props department."

"Told you," Cooper said smugly. Then his eyes lit up. "Look! It's Princess Aurora from Planet X! I've got to get her autograph!"

Ben tried to follow his friends, but he couldn't see very well through his monster mask. He bumped right into the strange device that Kevin was so curious about.

Whooooooooooosh!

The device lit up like a pinball machine. It hummed and wobbled. Then a tiny alien shot out of the front!

"Greetings," the alien said to Ben. "Are your people also planning to invade Earth? Because we thought of it first!"

Ben realized the alien thought he was an alien, too. "Uh, I'm just visiting," he lied. "Exactly what are you guys going to do?"

"The Laurians will take over this planet, one city at a time!" the alien cried. "We have fifty billion soldiers poised to attack."

Fifty billion? Ben wondered. That sounded hard to believe. Besides, if the rest of the Laurians were like this little guy, they should be easy to stop.

Blip! Another alien popped out of the machine. *Blip!* And another. *Blip! Blip! Blip!*

The machine was popping out aliens faster than Ben could count.

This could be a problem, Ben thought. He needed backup—and fast!

Ben took off his monster head and caught up to Kevin, Gwen, and Cooper. He quickly explained what had happened with the machine.

"Pretty soon this place is going to be crawling with aliens, and they've all got weapons," Ben said. "We've got to stop them."

"I'll get to work on the device," Cooper offered. Cooper was a technopath, which meant he could communicate with machines.

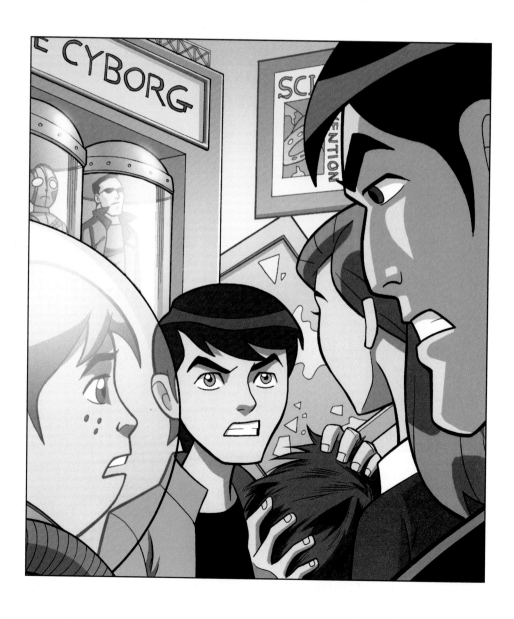

Ben turned the dials on his Ultimatrix. The small device he wore on his wrist contained the DNA codes for just about every life-form in the universe.

Green light washed over Ben as he transformed into the alien form he had dialed up.

"Echo Echo!"

An army of short, gray aliens with wide mouths appeared where Ben had just stood.

"Better Ultimize," said Ben in his Echo Echo form. He moved the dial once more.

"Ultimate Echo Echo!"

The tiny gray aliens became longer, bluer, and more powerful.

Ultimate Echo Echo chased a group of aliens into the Intergalactic Disco. The dancers screamed and ran as the Laurians started blasting them with their ray guns. Some of the Ultimate Echo Echoes quickly ushered the humans out through another door. Then they slammed the door shut, trapping the aliens inside.

The Laurians aimed their ray guns at the Ultimate Echo Echoes.

"We'll just blast our way out," one Laurian said.

A round, black amplifier detached from the body of each Ultimate Echo Echo. The floating amps surrounded the Laurians, blasting the aliens with a powerful sonic sound.

Stunned, the tiny aliens dropped their ray guns and fell to the floor.

Kevin chased a group of Laurians into the Alien Arcade.

Zap! Zap! Zap! The Laurians fired away at the convention goers.

Kevin grabbed onto a metal pole and absorbed the metal with his right hand.

"This oughta do it," Kevin guessed.
Bam! Bam! Bam! Kevin used his metal
hand like a mallet to bop the tiny aliens on the
head. One by one, they dropped to the floor.

Gwen found a group of Laurians attacking people in the food court. The greedy little aliens were gulping down drinks and gobbling up pizza.

Bursts of pink energy shot from Gwen's fingertips, surrounding the aliens. The bubbles lifted the Laurians into the air. The angry aliens zapped at the bubbles with their ray guns, popping them.

Gwen frowned—but she didn't give up.
This time, she aimed pink energy at a huge
tank of soda. She lifted the machine into the
air, dumping it on the Laurians. The sticky soda
doused the ray guns, and they fizzled out.

Meanwhile, some of the Laurians figured out that Cooper was trying to stop their machine.
"This Earthling is dangerous!" barked the Laurian leader. "Surround him!"
Oooooooooooeeeeeeeeeeeeeeeeee!

Across the convention hall, Ultimate Echo Echo fought off the Laurians with more sonic blasts. But the aliens seemed to be multiplying faster than he could take them down.

Then Cooper let out a yell.

"Help! Help! I'm under attack!"
Ben transformed back into his human
form and ran to help Cooper. Gwen and Kevin
arrived at the machine at the same time, just
as the aliens were carrying Cooper away.
"Cooper's the only one who can turn off
that machine," Gwen reminded everyone.

"Maybe not," Ben said. He dialed up another alien form on his Ultimatrix, then pressed the button. "Nanomech!"

This time, Ben transformed into one of his newest alien forms. Nanomech was part humanoid, part technology, and he could shrink to the size of a microchip.

Nanomech flew inside the machine. An electric charge sparked from his body as he communicated with the device.

"Cool," Nanomech said. "This thing goes in reverse!"

Nanomech reprogrammed the device from the inside.

Whooosh! The machine kicked into reverse, sucking the Laurians inside and sending them back to their planet.

Nanomech flew out of the machine and landed before the stunned faces of the convention goers. They watched, wide-eyed, as the machine sucked in the Laurians one by one.

Ben transformed. "Chill out, everybody!" he called out. "You just witnessed a stunt from this summer's biggest blockbuster, *Alien Invasion*. Right, Max?"

Max Kane played along. "R-r-right!" he stammered nervously. "This is exactly the kind of action you'll see in my new film!"

The sci-fi fans started texting immediately, getting the word out about *Alien Invasion*.

When things finally calmed down, Ben, Kevin, and Gwen took a break.

"It looks like *Alien Invasion* is going to be a huge hit," Gwen remarked.

"Yeah," Ben agreed. "But something tells me the movie won't be half as exciting as what just happened!"